Acting Edition

Fucking A

by Suzan-Lori Parks

I0591553

ǁSAMUEL FRENCHǁ

FOR PRODUCTION INQUIRIES

UNITED STATES AND CANADA
info@concordtheatricals.com
1-866-979-0447

UNITED KINGDOM AND EUROPE
licensing@concordtheatricals.co.uk
020-7054-7298

Each title is subject to availability from Concord Theatricals Corp.,
depending upon country of performance. Please be aware that
FUCKING A may not be licensed by Concord Theatricals Corp. in
your territory. Professional and amateur producers should contact the
nearest Concord Theatricals Corp. office or licensing partner to verify
availability.

FUCKING A was originally produced by DiverseWorks (Loris Bradley, Managing/Performing Arts Director) for Infernal Bridegroom Productions (Jason Nodler, Artistic Director) on February 24, 2000, in Houston, Texas. Funding was provided through a Rockefeller MAP Grant. The production was directed by the author. Scenic design was by Kirk Markley, with costume design by Danielle Wilton, lighting design by David Gipson and sound design by Douglas Robertson. Original lyrics and music were by Suzan-Lori Parks, musical direction and arrangement assistance were provided by Anthony Barilla, and the music was transcribed by Randall Eng. The cast was as follows:

HESTER SMITH	Tamarie Cooper
CANARY MARY	Amy Bruce
THE MAYOR	Charlie Scott
THE FIRST LADY	Amy Dickson
BUTCHER	Andy Nelson
MONSTER	Troy Schulze
FREEDOM FUND LADY	Lisa Marie Singerman
SCRIBE	Cary Winscott
FIRST HUNTER	Keith Reynolds
SECOND HUNTER	Alexander Marchand
THIRD HUNTER	Lisa Marie Singerman
JAILBAIT	Daniel Treadway
GUARD	Cary Winscott
WAITING WOMAN #1	Lisa Marie Singerman
WAITING WOMAN #2	Daniel Treadway
FRESHLY FREED PRISONERS	Daniel Treadway, Charlie Scott, Cary Winscott
TRANSLATOR	Cary Winscott

CHARACTERS

HESTER SMITH – the Abortionist

CANARY MARY – a friend of Hesters and a kept woman

THE MAYOR

THE FIRST LADY – his wife

BUTCHER

MONSTER

FREEDOM FUND LADY

SCRIBE

FIRST HUNTER

SECOND HUNTER

THIRD HUNTER

JAILBAIT

GUARD

WAITING WOMAN #1

WAITING WOMAN #2

3 FRESHLY FREED PRISONERS

AUTHOR'S NOTES

An otherworldly tale involving a noble Mother, her wayward Son, and others. Their troubled beginning, their difficult end. 19 scenes with songs.

The play calls for 11 actors with some doubling. The setting should be spare to reflect the poverty of the world of the play.

The play employs the foreign language of TALK. Translation for TALK may be found on page 104. The production should present a nonaudible simultaneous English translation.

FROM THE AUTHOR'S *ELEMENTS OF STYLE*

I'm continuing the use of my slightly unconventional theatrical elements. Here's a road map.

>   *(Rest)*

Take a little time, a pause, a breather; make a transition.

>   *A Spell*

An elongated and heightened *(Rest)*. Denoted by repetition of figures' names with no dialogue. Has sort of an architectural look:

> **CANARY.**
> **MONSTER.**
> **CANARY.**
> **MONSTER.**

This is a place where the figures experience their pure true simple state. While no action or stage business is necessary, directors should fill this moment as they best see fit.

>   *Parentheses*

Parentheses around dialogue indicate softly spoken passages (asides; sotto voce).

PART ONE

Scene One

(Hesters front room. Sparely furnished. A table, two chairs, and a wash bucket. This room functions as the main room of her home. There are two doors. One leads out the front. The other leads through her "workroom," and out the back. In a ceremonial altar-like place, two candles are burning. **HESTER** *walks into the room from the workroom, taking off her blood-spattered apron and hanging it on a hook, lighting another candle at the altar, then sitting at her wash bucket, wearily washing her tools clean. She wears a simple dress with an oddly cut-out square just above her left breast. There we can see the large "A" deeply branded into her skin. Bells announce the hour: midnight.)*

HESTER.

Midnight. Everyone should be in bed. But theyre not. Itd be nice if they was all in bed and not on their way to me. Cept the more they stay in bed the more they get in trouble. Then they gotta come to Hester for *die Abah-nazip.* 3 babys killed between the hours of 10 and midnight and at least one more before the nights out if I know whats what. Their troubles yr livlihood, Hester. Hhh. There aint no winning.

1

(A woman stands in her front doorway. Its
CANARY MARY *dressed in a bright yellow*
dress.)

CANARY.

Yr up.

HESTER.

Yr not. Yr the one should be in bed. Unless he dont
want you—

CANARY.

He wants me. More than ever. But tonight hes with his
wife.

HESTER.

The Bitch.

CANARY.

He says he owes it to the nation to give it one last shot.

HESTER.

May she rot.

CANARY.

Lookie. A present. Lookie—

HESTER.

Howbout some tea?

CANARY.

Howbout some booze. I got a story yll love.

HESTER.

Happy or sad?

CANARY.

Happy. So there we was—

HESTER.

I'd rather hear the sound of clinking coins. 5 coins a
week thats our deal. You got money but I always gotta
beg.

CANARY.

He gives me clothes, rarely cash.

(Rest)

Drink with me. Come on. Things are getting worse between the Mayor and his wife. Lets celebrate.

HESTER.

Cheers.

(They drink.)

CANARY.

The wifes at the end of her rope. He hates her. Her days are numbered.

HESTER.

But he loves her money so her money buys her time. The Rich Bitch.

CANARY.

This time its better. He says she makes his stomach churn. *Die la-sah Chung-chung? Sah Chung-chung lay schreck, lay frokum, lay woah woah crisp woah-ya.*

HESTER.

Rich Girl *seh tum woah Chung-chung crisp woah-ya,* Rich Girl!

CANARY.

Shes not the Rich Girl no more, shes our First Lady. You should give her respect.

HESTER.

First Lady *teeh tum-ay wee Kazo oromakeum*!

HESTER & CANARY.

Hahahahahahahahaha!

CANARY.

She dont got all the luck.

HESTER.

More luck than me.

CANARY.

Look—

HESTER.

May she rot—

CANARY.

Its a present.

HESTER.

—in the deepest pit for what she done to me and mine.

CANARY.

Lookie—

HESTER.

Not until my Boy comes home. Im not a true mother otherwise. When he comes home then maybe I'll forgive her but not before.

CANARY.

Look.

HESTER.

What.

CANARY.

Meat.

HESTER.

Fresh meat.

CANARY.

It was on yr doorstep.

HESTER.

On *my* doorstep?

CANARY.

Just sitting there. A present.

HESTER.

Its good meat.

CANARY.

Put it away so the flies wont get it.

HESTER.

It could be poison.

CANARY.

Put it away and tomorrow cook it up and invite me over. Go on.

(Rest)

No one would wanna kill you. We need you too much. Like me, you perform one of those disrespectable but most necessary services.

HESTER.

Me in my bloody apron. You in yr yellow dress.

CANARY.

You like it? Its new. Im getting shoes to go with it.

HESTER.

It makes you look like a whore.

CANARY.

I am a whore.

HESTER.

Yr a kept woman.

CANARY.

Im a whore. Yr an abortionist Im a whore.

HESTER.

Cheers.

(Rest)

If Im lucky by the end of next year I'll have paid enough for me and Boy to have a reunion picnic. Thatll take 500 coins.

CANARY.

One gold piece. Thats a lot.

HESTER.

I'll make it, yll see

(Rest)

Who knows what he looks like now. Hes alive. Freedom Fund assures me of that. All growd up, thats for sure. And tall. And a beard. And a deep voice. And a smile in his eye like his dad had and—

CANARY.

Handsome.

HESTER.

If he takes after his dad hes good looking but dont you go getting any ideas. Hes a good boy and when I finally buy his freedom he'll be looking for a wife. He wont want the likes of you.

CANARY.

The Mayor owns my exclusive rights so I wouldnt have no time for a poor man even if he was handsome. Although poor men got a beauty to them. But nope. The son of an abortionist. I'd turn my nose up.

HESTER.

Whore.

CANARY.

Babykiller.

(They sing "Working Womans Song.")

HESTER & CANARY.

ITS NOT THAT WE LOVE
WHAT WE DO,
BUT WE DO IT.
WE LOOK AT THE DAY,
WE JUST GOTTA GET THROUGH IT.
WE DIG OUR DITCH WITH NO COMPLAINING,
WORK IN HOT SUN, OR EVEN WHEN ITS RAINING,
AND WHEN THE LONG DAY FINALLY COMES TO AN END,
WE'LL SAY:
"HERE IS A WOMAN
WHO DOES ALL SHE CAN."

CANARY.

So there I was—

HESTER.

A letter came from Boy today. Its right here. Read it to me?

CANARY.

In a minute. Thisll make you smile. Its at her expense.

HESTER.

Go on.

CANARY.

There I was in his bed. I was in his bed and he was on top of me and we was going at it, right? And we was screaming and carrying on like we always do. At first we used to be so quiet out of respect for her—

HESTER.

The Bitch—

CANARY.

Exactly. But now she aint given Hizzoner an heir or heiress neither so what does he owe her, right? So we scream and carry on when we go at it. And for some reason she walks right into the room. And the Mayor and me is making so much noise that neither of us hear her. And she is standing right beside the bed and, you know I got my eyes open I always do it with my eyes open cause I like to watch him enjoy, and there she is standing there. Watching. And I look at her. And Hizzoner sees me looking at something and he turns his head, without a break in his screwing stride, right, he turns his head and looks at her. Just stares at her and keeps on screwing me. And they looked at each other like that. It was some kind of standoff. Him screwing me and staring at her and her staring at him and me looking back and forth from his face to her face. Then she bursts into tears and runs out of the room.

HESTER.

Serves her right.

CANARY.

Shes the only woman in the whole country who cant seem to get knocked up. Ordinarily I'd feel sorry for a woman in her position but—All that time she spent in *Europe*. All those *doctors* she seen. The mounds of drugs she takes. Nothing works. Every month *falltima Ovo ella greek Tragedy woah-ya.*

HESTER.

When she was a little Rich Girl she thought she owned the world. And anything she wanted she could buy.

Sent my son away to prison with a flick of her little Rich Girl finger. She cant buy a son or a daughter now but I can buy mine. Im buying mine back.

(Rest)

Read the letter.

CANARY.

The Mayor says hes going to bump her off. Bump her off and keep her money.

HESTER.

Her just desserts.

CANARY.

Then he'll marry me he says.

HESTER.

You love him?

CANARY.

No. But he buys me anything I want.

(Rest)

Yll still be my best friend dont worry. I'll still come around. Even though you stink.

HESTER.

Only when a customer is on her way.

CANARY.

Then one must be coming.

HESTER.

Hmm. The only thing worse than a branded A is a stinking weeping one.

CANARY.

Im used to it.

> *(**HESTERS** old wound, the large branded A above her left breast, weeps as a fresh wound would.)*

HESTER.

The A looks so fresh, like they branded me just yesterday.

(Rest)

I'll put on my apron. She'll be here in a minute. You better go.

(**HESTER** *readies for work.*)

CANARY.
CANARY.
CANARY.

(Rest)

CANARY.
You helped me out years ago. You didnt even know me. I couldnt afford *die Abah-nazip*. You said I could pay you back whenever.

HESTER.
And Im getting my fee plus the interest. Im a good business woman.

CANARY.
Yr a good friend.

HESTER.
Dont overdo it.

CANARY.
Here. My debt and then some.

(**CANARY** *gives her a gold coin.*)

HESTER.
A gold coin.

CANARY.
Enough for that picnic.

HESTER.
I'll see him this week! Canary!

CANARY.
Dont hug me too hard. Oh dry yr eyes, Im feeling stupid.

HESTER.

Thank you.

CANARY.

Customers not here yet. Howabout I read a little.

(**CANARY** *gets the letter, opens it, and reads it to* **HESTER** *as the lights fade.*)

"Dear Mother. How are you? I am fine. I am doing my very best to be a good son but it is difficult to be good when surrounded by so much bad. I got two weeks time in the hold last month. No sunlight no food only water. I would tell you why I got the time but what I did was bad. But I did it to a bad person, so that aint so bad is it?..."

Scene Two

(The **MAYOR** and the **FIRST LADY** in the
middle of a conversation.)

FIRST LADY.

Aaaaaaaaaaaaaaaaaaaaaaaaah! *Papameh! Falltimeh
ma-Ovo!* Aaaaaaaaaaaaaaaaaah!

MAYOR.

Scream cry rant rave threaten me curse me denounce
me place blame gimmie the finger thumb yr nose
tear yr hair out tear my hair out kick the dog kick the
servants have some of the poor bumped off yell weep
sob moan blubber stomp yr feet curse the gods tell yr
father but remind him that not only do I have the army
behind me but I answer to the people. I must answer to
the people. And those people elected me to lead. And
those people elected me to lead for the rest of my life
and when they elected me they expected me to produce
a son and they elected and expected that son to lead for
the rest of his life and so on and so on and so on and so
on and so on and—

FIRST LADY.

My father will—

MAYOR.

Your father will nothing. He finds your inability
disgraceful.

FIRST LADY.

Im yr wife.

MAYOR.

And Im the Mayor. The people look up to me. They
look up to me and they see my right hand dangling.
Where I should be holding the hand of my son, or
perhaps have my arm resting proudly on the young
mans shoulder my right hand is only dangling. Empty.
And they see it. And they begin to wonder what kind
of man I am. I promised them a greatness that would

last a hundred-thousand years but my right hand is
dangling empty, Woman.

FIRST LADY.

Ive tried. I went to *Europe*. Saw all those doctors. All
of them poking at me. All of them overcharging me
because they all knew I was foreign. All the pills they
gave me. Suitcases full. And I take them. I take them
every day. Ive tried.

MAYOR.

Yr trying is trying the patience of the people. I cant
make any more excuses for you.

FIRST LADY.

But you could spend more time with me. *Meh Kazo-say
greengrass ee-sunny skies ee—*

MAYOR.

And ineffective.

(Rest)

Ive been thoroughly examined. Theres no question as
to my effectiveness. I must say I was proud when, after
an initially embarrassing moment, the mock-sexual
experience into the paper cup (dont kid yrself I didnt
think of you while I was at it). How embarrassing it all
was. But then to see, under the microscope, all those
little men swimming. An army! My own little private
army!

*(The **MAYOR** sings "My Little Army.")*

MAYOR.

LOYALTY IS THE MOST IMPORTANT THING IN AN ARMY
AND MY MEN HAVE LOYALTY TO ME.
THEY WILL LAY DOWN THEIR LIVES
SO OUR STATE WILL SURVIVE.
I FIND THAT KIND OF COURAGE VERY CHARMING.
I SALUTE THE MEN OF MY
LITTLE ARMY.

MAYOR.

The people see your inability as a kind of treason.

FIRST LADY.

We're not at war.

MAYOR.

But we could be. One day.

FIRST LADY.

We are a small town in a small country in the middle of nowhere. Small towns in small countries dont go to war.

MAYOR.

That kind of thinking is the kind of thinking that keeps us back. Born with a silver spoon in yr mouth never had to work so its no wonder you dont produce.

(Rest)

Yr a disgrace to the nation. Everyone agrees. I should remove you from our townhouse and put you in our country house.

FIRST LADY.

Send me to the country house and when everyones forgotten me, yll have one of yr flunkies slit my throat.

MAYOR.

The people think a rest in the country may help you. Yll have a few days to pack yr things. My hands are tied. Im sorry. Wheres my basket?

FIRST LADY.

Right there.

(Rest)

Where are you going?

MAYOR.

My weekly errands. The Mayor rubs shoulders with the people. After all these years they still like it.

FIRST LADY.

One more shot. Please. Just one more.

MAYOR.

I have errands.

FIRST LADY.

Please.

(Rest)

Think of the nation.

FIRST LADY.

Mayor

MAYOR.

Fine.

FIRST LADY.
MAYOR.

MAYOR.

Come on, lets get going.

> *(She begins to kiss and seduce him. She is more passionate than he.)*

Scene Three

(**HESTER** *at the* **FREEDOM FUND**. *She states her case to the* **FREEDOM FUND LADY**.)

FREEDOM FUND.

His files here somewhere. Not to worry. We never lose anything. Of course you could just make a payment get a receipt and I could enter it all into his file at a later time.

HESTER.

I dont mind waiting. Todays special. Im paying extra.

FREEDOM FUND.

Paying extra! Wonderful. "Freedom Aint Free!" Glad you understand our motto, Mrs. Smith.

(Rest)

Now lets see. Last name Smith first name Boy. BoySmith BoySmith BoySmith. Its in here somewhere.

(Rest)

Look at yr A.

(Rest)

Yr an Abortionist.

HESTER.

Obviously.

FREEDOM FUND.

Whats it like?

HESTER.

Hard.

FREEDOM FUND.

"Someones gotta empty the toilet!" so they say. Mrs. Smith, Abortionist. Working hard at what you do. Yr distressing occupation. Ive never had a need of yr services, but I did have a friend once who came to you. The public clinic had a looong wait list—yr quick and you do the job for half the price. Said you were very thorough. And that yr the most discreet woman in the country. Thats something.

(Rest)

You know there are lots of women coming through this place in need of *die Abah-nazip*. They got a man in jail or a dead-beat lover or no money for another kid. Some women, Mrs. Smith, lemmie tell you, *tee-tee kop fuh Binah Zoo.*

HESTER.

Hee la Mau Chungwoah nice-like.

FREEDOM FUND.

Hi! Hi! Hi-Chungwoah! Teeh Kazohi-woah-ya tutti may Baza.

HESTER.

Woah-ya dahteh.

FREEDOM FUND.

But what can you do? And them cleaning up their act would put you out of yr cleaning business.

(Rest)

What did you do before you started—doing what yr doing now?

HESTER.

Scrubbed floors for the Rich Family but then Boy stole from them and they came down extra extra hard on me. It was either prison or—

FREEDOM FUND.

And a mother cant buy her sons freedom in prison. You chose employment, Mrs. Smith. Youve got initiative. Thats good.

HESTER.

Thank you.

*(**FREEDOM FUND** finally finds the file.)*

FREEDOM FUND.

Well. Boy Smith. Here he is! Youve been making steady payments. Thats admirable. A prisoner can sense when his family is making steady payments. It gives them hope. How much ya paying today?

HESTER.

A gold coin.

FREEDOM FUND.

A gold coin! Hand it here! Gold!

HESTER.

I look forward to picnicking with my Boy this week.

FREEDOM FUND.

Not so fast! Not so fast!

(Rest)

First lets log this in the book and put it in the bank. Gold. And of course log it in his file. Now lets see where it puts you! Yr a hard-working mother Mrs. Smith.

HESTER.

I am.

FREEDOM FUND.

Oh dear.

(Rest)

Hes committed a few crimes since yr last payment.

HESTER.

Must be a mistake. Hes a very good boy

FREEDOM FUND.

Of course he is. Its just that. Well, yr good boys been doing some very bad things lately.

HESTER.

When we have our picnic I'll tell him—

FREEDOM FUND.

Picnic. Picnic. Picnic. Yr son wont be up for a picnic any time soon. His picnic price has doubled.

HESTER.

Doubled?

FREEDOM FUND.

Im sorry.

HESTER.

If only that Rich Little Bitch hadnt told on him! We worked for them. They treated us worse than animals. He was only hungry! He stole some meat and she seen him and he seen her seeing him and begged her not to tell, one child to another, but she told. Went and snitched on my Boy and they took him away.

(Rest)

His price couldnt of doubled, maam.

FREEDOM FUND.

Im sorry.

HESTER.

Its all that Rich Girls fault.

FREEDOM FUND.

You cant blame her for his current incarceration. His initial three year sentence has doubled and trippled and quadrupled and—since hes been in jail hes committed several crimes.

HESTER.

He tells me everything. Those crimes are frame-ups every one of them.

FREEDOM FUND.

Hes a hardened criminal, Mrs. Smith.

HESTER.

My sons an angel.

FREEDOM FUND.

Angels fall.

HESTER.

No.

(Rest)

Ive just miscalculated his picnic price is all. Silly me.

(Rest)

Hes a good boy, maam. A very good boy.

> (**HESTER** *leaves.*)

Scene Four

(A park bench in the middle of nowhere overlooking the sea. MONSTER just sits there. After a moment CANARY MARY comes by. They sit and watch the sea. MONSTER looks her over surreptitiously.)

MONSTER.
Nice view.

MONSTER.
CANARY.

MONSTER.
Nice dress.

MONSTER.
CANARY.

MONSTER.
Come here often?

CANARY.
MONSTER.
CANARY.
MONSTER.

CANARY.
You dont look familiar.
MONSTER.
Im not. Im new. New in town.
CANARY.
Towns that way. About a mile.
MONSTER.
Im in no hurry to see it. Its nice here. The sea. The air. The sun.

CANARY.
    The quiet.
MONSTER.
    Right.

CANARY.
MONSTER.
CANARY.
MONSTER.

MONSTER.
    Whatcha reading?
CANARY.
    Words.

    (Rest)

    Wow. Yr arm. Thats some birthmark.
MONSTER.
    Its a scar. From a long time ago.
CANARY.
    Does it hurt?
MONSTER.
    It did. Not no more.

    (Rest)

    I was in prison.
CANARY.
    Prison?
MONSTER.
    Years ago. Someone cut me. It hurt at first. Not no
    more.

MONSTER.
CANARY.

MONSTER.

I heard this was a good place to meet women. They told the truth cause here you are.

(Rest)

Can I kiss you?

CANARY.

My lovers rich. He owns exclusive rights to me.

MONSTER.

Oh.

CANARY.

Yeah.

(Rest)

Yr cute. Good luck.

(She goes on her way. He watches her go.)

Scene Five

(In the tavern. **SCRIBE** *and* **BUTCHER.***)*

BUTCHER.

You drunk? Scribe?

SCRIBE.

What.

BUTCHER.

You drunk?

SCRIBE.

Yeah.

BUTCHER.

You been drunk all week.

SCRIBE.

Yeah.

BUTCHER.

You got someone writing in yr stead?

SCRIBE.

Nope.

BUTCHER.
SCRIBE.

SCRIBE.

You know when I first learned to write?

BUTCHER.

When you were 3 years old.

SCRIBE.

Howd you know that?

BUTCHER.

Ive known you all yr life.

SCRIBE.

We grew up together, you and me. Next door neighbors.
In the hills.

BUTCHER.

Lets get you home.

SCRIBE.

Dad wanted me to make something of myself. So he stood over me with a stick. I still got the welts, well, the scars of the welts.

(Rest)

Perfectly formed letters at 3 years old. The most beautiful alphabet you ever seen. You seen it, Butcher, right? You seen it, right? I got it hanging—

BUTCHER.

On the wall in yr shop. Lets go. You can show it to me.

SCRIBE.

Naw.

BUTCHER.

Theres lots of people wanting writing done and yr shops closed. Thats bad business.

SCRIBE.

Butcher. It took me a whole week to get this drunk. Don't ruin it. Toast.

> **(SCRIBE** *toasts and drinks all by himself.*
> **3 HUNTERS** *come in.)*

FIRST HUNTER.

I shoulda gotten his balls! I shoulda gotten his balls! Im telling you I shoulda gotten his balls!

SECOND HUNTER.

You werent the first to eye him.

FIRST HUNTER.

I didnt eye him first but I was the first to say: "There he is!"

THIRD HUNTER.

"There he is," so what?! Harry was pointing right at him. We all *knew* where he was.

FIRST HUNTER.

　　But my saying it out loud alerted the dogs.

SECOND HUNTER.

　　You have a point.

THIRD HUNTER.

　　Harrys pointing alerted the dogs. When he pointed they all jerked their heads up in the air.

SECOND HUNTER.

　　But they didnt charge till Hank said: "There he is."

FIRST HUNTER.

　　Which means I shoulda got the bastard convicts balls.

THIRD HUNTER.

　　You got the bastards feet. Thats second place. Feet arent so bad.

FIRST HUNTER.

　　I guess.

　　(Rest)

　　They should let us keep the heads.

SECOND HUNTER.

　　Then howd we prove we'd caught anything?

FIRST HUNTER.

　　You got a point.

　　(Rest)

　　Hey, Butcher!

BUTCHER.

　　Hey, Hank. Hal. Harv.

FIRST HUNTER.

　　Scribe?

BUTCHER.

　　Loaded.

THIRD HUNTER.

　　All I got was a finger. Off the *left* hand. My wife thinks Im a loser.

SECOND HUNTER.

What can you do.

FIRST HUNTER.

He screamed good, though didnt he?

THIRD HUNTER.

I can still hear it in my head. When Homer put the coals in his chest—

SECOND HUNTER.

"Why you doing this to me why you doing this to me?!" he was screaming. Like he didnt know us Hunters was gonna be on his trail when he escaped.

FIRST HUNTER.

He was a nobody. Wish he'd been a famous convict. The prizes woulda been worth more and the pay woulda been better.

SECOND HUNTER.

One of my dogs broke its leg or something.

THIRD HUNTER.

I'll take a look at it later.

SECOND HUNTER.

I'd appreciate it.

(They sing the "The Hunters Creed.")

HUNTERS.

WE HUNT,
BUT WE DO
NOT
EAT WHAT WE CATCH.
THATD BE A LITTLE MUCH,
DONTCHA THINK?
WE HUNT,
BUT WE DO
NOT
EAT WHAT WE CATCH.
THATD BE A LITTLE MUCH,
DONTCHA THINK?

FIRST HUNTER.

Drinks on me.

(He goes and gets a bottle.)

SECOND HUNTER.

Hows business?

BUTCHER.

Like yours. Lots of work and nothing to show. The Knife Catalog came this morning.

THIRD HUNTER.

Bring it over.

FIRST HUNTER.

Word is they had a convict escape up north two nights ago. Someone wholl bring a good price too. "Monster" they call him. "Monster"! Hes pure evil. Done everything bad there is to do. Heres the paper, give it a read.

THIRD HUNTER.

Murder, necrophilia, sodomy, bestiality, pedophilia, armed robbery, petty theft, embezzlement, diddling in public, cannibalism—

SECOND HUNTER.

Whew.

FIRST HUNTER.

Makes you sick, dont it?

SECOND HUNTER.

Yeah.

FIRST HUNTER.

"Monster"!

THIRD HUNTER.

Just our luck though. He got out up north, we wont have a chance at spotting him down here.

BUTCHER.

Look at that blade Hank.

FIRST HUNTER.

Thats some blade.

SECOND HUNTER.

Maybe the convictll come down here. All them boats we got going to *Europe*. Maybe the convict wants to go to *Europe*.

THIRD HUNTER.

He wont be wanting to go to *Europe*. He'll be wanting to hide in the hills. In the northern hills.

FIRST HUNTER.

"Monster"! Ha!

SECOND HUNTER.

Shit thats some blade Butcher.

BUTCHER.

Show that to a pig and its skinll go Red Sea just at the sight of it.

SECOND HUNTER.

Wow.

THIRD HUNTER.

Flip to the back, lets see whats on sale.

FIRST HUNTER.

I bet "Monster" comes down here.

SECOND HUNTER.

How much you betting?

FIRST HUNTER.

How much you got?

> (**SECOND HUNTER** *digs through his pockets counting his money.* **HESTER** *comes in. She stands off to the side, a good distance from them, looking through the crowd for the* **SCRIBE.***)*

SECOND HUNTER.

I got 12 coins. 12 coins says he aint coming.

HUNTERS.
HESTER.
HUNTERS.

HESTER.

I come in for the Scribe. He aint been at his stand all week. Scribe?

THIRD HUNTER.

Wait for him outside. Yr stinking up the place.

HESTER.

Ive been waiting. Hey, Scribe, I got an important letter you gotta write.

SECOND HUNTER.

Tough luck, Stinky.

FIRST HUNTER.

Cover up yr A or something.

HESTER.

I cant its against the law.

THIRD HUNTER.

Pweeeeeeewwww!

BUTCHER.

Harv, leave her be.

FIRST HUNTER.

Shes a babykiller. Thats what she is.

HESTER.

Yr daughters been a customer of mine. More than once.

FIRST HUNTER.

Shut yr trap!

HESTER.

Le doe-dunk eyesee Frahla ehle dunk sehh Frahla ah ma, Mister Hunter.

SECOND HUNTER.

Thats private family business. I'll smash yr face for blabbing that!

BUTCHER.

Hal! Hey! You got better things to do than hit a woman.

SECOND HUNTER.
BUTCHER.

FIRST HUNTER.

Didnt know you spoke TALK.

SECOND HUNTER.

Just enough to get by.

FIRST HUNTER.

My wife wants me to learn it but I say no way. Keep that stuff private. Like it should be. Thats what I say.

SECOND HUNTER.
BUTCHER.

THIRD HUNTER.

10 coins says the convictll come our way. Another 3 says I'll sight him first.

FIRST HUNTER.

Drinks on me!

BUTCHER.

Come on, Scribe. You got work to do.

(Rest)

He'll get up in a minute.

HESTER.

I'll wait outside.

> (**HESTER** *goes outside.* **BUTCHER** *helps* **SCRIBE** *to his feet. The* **HUNTERS** *sing their song again.)*

HUNTERS.

WE HUNT,
BUT WE DO
NOT
EAT WHAT WE CATCH.
THATD BE A LITTLE MUCH,
DONTCHA THINK?
WE HUNT,
BUT WE DO

NOT
EAT WHAT WE CATCH.
THATD BE A LITTLE MUCH,
DONTCHA THINK?

Scene Six

(**HESTER** *walks along the street with her freshly written letter.*)

HESTER.

"Darling Son," it says. "Its spring again and so Im outside scrubbing the marble walk. Every day I wake at dawn and scrub. The same walkway Ive scrubbed every spring since we went to work for them. They arent as mean as when we worked here together. Ive got plenty to eat and hope you do too. Love, Ma." Wish I had enough coins to include more. Well. This is good enough. Next year we'll be picnicking. We'll have meat and cheese and wine and bread and apples.

(Rest)

No shame in telling a lie. "I still work for the Rich People." Ha! Better to lie than to have him ashamed cause his mothers a babykiller.

(Rest)

"Darling Son!" it says, "Its spring again and so Im—"

(*The* **FIRST LADY** *passes by. She tries to dodge* **HESTER** *but* **HESTER** *confronts her.*)

HESTER.
FIRST LADY.

HESTER.

Bitch.

FIRST LADY.

Excuse me.

HESTER.

Bitch. I hear hes sending you away! You deserve it!

(*The* **FIRST LADY** *hurries on her way as* **HESTER** *shouts curses at her.*)

HESTER.

*Suptah nekkie frokrisp Chung-chung! Noonka Bleehc
tryohla die. Noonka! Grope tillie not. Grope say Basket
shreck eey grope say winduptrala! Grope sah Tupdom
linke die like um die Nassum. Grope sah Ovoweh miss
eeh so quaknie! Grope sah Milch shreck eeh naymilch
noonkey treben! Noonke!*

> *(After spending her anger, **HESTER** pauses to
> catch her breath and then continues on her
> way.)*

Scene Seven

(The **MAYOR** *fully dressed.* **CANARY** *in her underwear.* **MAYOR** *takes off his clothes.* **CANARY** *angrily gets dressed.)*

*(***MAYOR*** *gets dressed.)*

MAYOR.

Yr sore.

CANARY.

Im not sore.

MAYOR.

Good. Get naked.

(She takes off her clothes. As he gets partly undressed, she gets partly dressed.)

CANARY.
MAYOR.

CANARY.

I'd like a ring. A ring aint too much to ask.

MAYOR.

I told her to go to the country but she wont go. She knows whats up.

CANARY.

Ring Ring! Ring Ring!

(Rest)

Yr tired of me.

MAYOR.

I cant think of rings right now.

(Rest)

Planning a murder takes a lot of thought. Shes got to be wiped out just right so that the blame falls on some

nobody and not at all on me or my office. Ive got to be
kept in the clear.

CANARY.

Have one of yr lieutenants do it. Or a sniper. I'll do it if
you want.

MAYOR.

You would?

CANARY.

One of yr lieutenants would make it more—
professional.

MAYOR.

Yr right.

CANARY.

She'll be dead. Yll weep at her funeral. Yll get all her
money. Yll marry me.

MAYOR.

My wife will die a tragic death. I will stand like the
soldier that I am as they put her in the deep dark
ground. My chest will heave in sadness but no tears will
fall. I am their soldier-Mayor. Not a tear will fall. She
will have left me all her money. I will hang my head
and the people will want me to lift my head up. The
people will demand that I remarry.

(Rest)

They will demand that I remarry a woman of a—of a
certain background. My heart will be split in two. Each
night with my new wife I will dream of you. I am their
humble civil servant. I cannot let them down.

CANARY.

You will let them down by replacing one *kaltie Bleehc*
with another.

MAYOR.

As their Mayor Im prepared to sacrifice my pleasure.
Besides. Nothing between us will change. I'll be
remarried. And in good time I'll be a father, so I'll be
more relaxed. But nothing between us will change.

CANARY.

You said youd marry me.

(Rest)

You gave your word.

(Rest)

I love you.

MAYOR.

I have the future of my country to consider.

CANARY.

You are the Mayor they are the people. You are the shepherd they are the sheep. You set the clock you style the fashion you define the taste.

MAYOR.

They elected me—

CANARY.

To rule for a hundred thousand years.

MAYOR.

How many days is that? How many hours how many minutes.

CANARY.

How many kisses?

(Rest)

Marry me.

(Rest)

Im begging on my knees.

MAYOR.
CANARY.
MAYOR.
CANARY.

MAYOR.

Heres some gold.

MAYOR.
CANARY.

MAYOR.

"Wife," "Mistress," what does it matter? Take the gold.
Buy something nice.

> *(He gives her several gold coins.)*

CANARY.

Sweetheart.

MAYOR.

Good girl.

> *(A gentle moment then she steps away. She
> sings "Gilded Cage.")*

CANARY.

I DREAMED I MET A LIONESS
SHE ONCE LIVED IN THE WILD,
SHE ONCE HUNTED FOR ALL HER FOOD,
SHE ONCE WAS SO SELF-STYLED.
SHE ONCE ROAMED ANYWHERE SHE PLEASED,
SHE ONCE WAS FREE AND BRAVE.
BUT IN MY DREAM SHE SPOKE TO ME
FROM A GORGEOUS GILDED CAGE.

HER GILDED CAGE WAS SOLID GOLD,
THE BARS SHONE LIKE SUNSHINE.
SHE'D GONE IN THERE ALL ON HER OWN,
NO ONE HAD FORCED HER
THIS TIME.
"FREEDOM," SHE SAID, "AINT FREE AT ALL.
ITS PRICE: A HEAVY WAGE.
AND WHEN YOU FIND HOW MUCH YOUR FREEDOM
    COSTS,
YOU JUST MAY GIVE IT UP
FOR A GORGEOUS GILDED CAGE."

Scene Eight

*(That park bench in the middle of nowhere
overlooking the sea. The* **FIRST LADY** *sits there
crying. After a moment* **MONSTER** *comes by.
He looks her over surreptitiously then sits
and watches the sea. She notices him and
composes herself.)*

MONSTER.
FIRST LADY.

MONSTER.
    Nice view.

MONSTER.
FIRST LADY.

MONSTER.
    Nice dress.

MONSTER.
FIRST LADY.

MONSTER.
    Come here often?

FIRST LADY.
MONSTER.
FIRST LADY.
MONSTER.

FIRST LADY.
    Im sad.
MONSTER.
    Im not.

(Rest)

Im new. New in town.

FIRST LADY.

Im sad.

MONSTER.

Yr beautiful.

(Rest)

Beautiful like the ocean only the ocean is moving and you are. Still.

(Rest)

I always wanted to meet a woman like that.

FIRST LADY.

My husband doesnt want me.

MONSTER.

Cant be true. Someone as beautiful as you.

FIRST LADY.
MONSTER.

FIRST LADY.

Gosh. Yr arm. Thats some birthmark.

MONSTER.

Its a scar. From a long time ago.

FIRST LADY.

Does it hurt?

MONSTER.

It did. Not no more.

(Rest)

Thats the trick with things that hurt. Outlast them, they stop hurting. Sooner or later.

FIRST LADY.

You think?

MONSTER.

Thats been my experience.

FIRST LADY.
MONSTER.
FIRST LADY.
MONSTER.

FIRST LADY.
    May I kiss you?

        (She kisses him. They kiss.)

Scene Nine

(Hesters home. Late at night. The room is dark. She comes in through the back door. Shes wearing her bloody apron, having just finished another abortion. She throws her tools into the wash bucket and, going over to the altar-like place, lights a candle. The candle illuminates the room and she sees someone sitting there: **BUTCHER***, also in his bloody apron.)*

HESTER.

Butcher. Well. Its late.

BUTCHER.

You should lock your door. Theres another convict on the loose.

HESTER.

Most people think its bad luck coming here.

(Rest)

Yll have bad luck now.

BUTCHER.

I got bad luck already.

HESTER.
BUTCHER.

HESTER.

I must be way behind in my meat bill. I know yr a man who likes his customers to pay their bills on time.

BUTCHER.

Hester—

HESTER.

Freedom comes first. I pay the Freeodom Fund on time, or they add on extra. They miscalculated recently.

It really set me back. But ha! I came into some more money earlier today. Another wonderful gift from a very good friend. I guess you heard about it and are here looking for whats owed you but Im going to the Fund again tomorrow and pay on my sons freedom. Its not enough to spring him but this time for sure itll get us the picnic lunch. For sure this time. Ive checked and rechecked the figures. This time for sure we'll be eating together by the end of the week. Me and Boy. After 30 years. You gotta understand, my meat bills—

BUTCHER.

Zero. You dont owe.

HESTER.

Oh.

(Rest)

BUTCHER.

Canary give you the money?

HESTER.

Yes. Another gold coin. Just a little while ago. She really wants to help out.

BUTCHER.

Thats good of her.

HESTER.

Shes a good friend.

HESTER.
BUTCHER.

BUTCHER.

Sit. Sit with me.

> *(She sits. Theyre both sitting there in their bloody aprons.)*

BUTCHER.

It was nice seeing you the other day.

HESTER.

> Scribe wrote me a good letter. Thanks for getting him
> on his feet.

HESTER.
BUTCHER.

HESTER.

> He makes the nicest looking letters. Even when hes
> sloshed. Such pretty shapes, straight bold lines and
> gentle curls. Makes me wish I could read. And write
> too.

BUTCHER.

> You should learn.

HESTER.

> Well.

BUTCHER.

> Its not that hard. I could teach you.
>
> *(Rest)*
>
> If you learned writing you could write yr son yrself,
> save money on Scribe and spend less time working.
>
> *(Rest)*
>
> And I'd be happy to teach you. Itd be my pleasure.

HESTER.
BUTCHER.

HESTER.

> You got a daughter locked up too, dontcha?

BUTCHER.

> Shes a bad seed.

HESTER.

> Its hard to be good when surrounded by so many bad
> people.

BUTCHER.

My kid, Lulu. Rotten to the core she is. Always was. From day one, that Lulu. She was always into something bad.

(Rest)

[Prostitution, racketeering, moneylaundering, cyber fraud, intellectual embezzlement, highway robbery, dialing for dollars, doing a buffalo after midnight, printing her own money, cheating at cheating, jaywalking, selling herself without a license, selling her children without a permit, unlawful reproduction, having more than one spouse, claiming to have multiple parents, claiming to have multiple orgasms, claiming to have injuries she didnt have, claiming to have been places she never was, making love at gunpoint, indecent exposure, hanging upside down in a public place, walking in the rain without a flashlight, walking home from work without a pink slip, taking up more than one seat of the public conveyance, not saluting the authorities, having no known address, skipping school, skipping her monthly, smoking in the girls room, drugging of all stripes and varieties, taking and dispensing narcotics without a permit, smiling in the off season, hunting on private land, lying on private grass, trespassing, eating from the table of authority, fornicating with the Other, overdue shit at the LendingSpot, general physical underdevelopment, looking up too much, looking into the eyes of her arresting authority, taking a crap in the office of said arresting authority, playing with herself on the governments nickel, aiding and abetting a whole host of things, admitting to participating in a boondoggle, running red lights, general dismemberment, congregating without a permit, speaking her mind without a permit, not wearing drawers, leaving her lights on, playing loud music, fighting the power, passing the buck, not paying the electric, obscene phone calls, ringing and running, conversations with children who were not her own thus implanting strange notions in the minds of minors, conversations with adults which bordered on the ridiculous, fornicating with the same sex, fornicating with young men under the age of 15 and old men over the age of her old mans age, saying she was married when she wasnt, having no sense of direction, grand larceny, petty theft, hotwiring, image manipulation, leading unsuspecting men and women into cyberspace and leaving them there lost and without a roadmap, riding without a helmet, fraternizing with known felons, copulating with said known felons with the intent to reproduce, espionage, high treason, mutiny at sea, operating a dumptruck without a license, having improper identification, slave trading, horse stealing, murder in the first degree, not knowing what time it is, talking too much, laughing out of turn, murder in the second degree, standing on one leg in a 2-legged zone, jumping the turnstile, jumping the turnstilee, burning down the house, murder in the nth degree, failing to perform life-saving procedures in a situation that warranted it, aiding and abetting a forest fire, failing to predict a series of natural disasters, perjury, not pulling her weight, not wearing her teeth, fingering the Commander, selling state secrets, not believing in The Afterlife, defaming the name of the State, passing as a persona non grata, defacing animates and intimates alike, persuading, dumping pollutants, not doing her bit, having neither gimmick nor schtick, mugging i.e. pulling faces, mugging i.e. sticking up—you get the gist—having bad timing, possessing a firearm, not eating her vegetables, being a bad apple, falling too far from the tree, possessing a concealed freakish attribute, harboring the convicted, fencing the stolen, giving false testimony, raising the dead, envisioning the future, remembering the past, speeding—huh.

(Rest)

(Rest)

HESTER.

Impressive.]

BUTCHER.

Shes not eligible for the Freedom Fund Program.

HESTER.

I wouldnt think she would be.

(Rest)

My Boys an angel who had a little bad luck.

BUTCHER.

Thats life.

HESTER.

BUTCHER.

BUTCHER.

Butcherings the only thing I ever wanted to do. I feel like Im right in the middle of the great chain of being. Passing life from one group to another. Sure I kill them but I make sure it never hurts. Ive spent all my life perfecting the painless slaughter. Lemmie show you.

(With his sheathed knife in hand he comes to her, standing behind her, putting the knife near her throat, instructing her.)

BUTCHER.

Yr slaughtering a pig. Smart animal. Also very bloody. You put him between yr legs with his back toward you. Lift up his head and quick! Slice quick. They cry out but its only reflex. Ive read all the anatomy books. This kind of cut is completely painless.

(Rest)

You try.

*(They switch places. **HESTER** gives it a try.)*

HESTER.

Like this?

BUTCHER.

Faster and dont bear down so hard. The knife is sharp.
You dont want him feeling a thing. Like the cold wind
crossed his throat, thats all.

HESTER.

Like this?

BUTCHER.

Thats it. Once more.

HESTER.

Ha!

BUTCHER.

Good Job!

HESTER.

Thank you.

BUTCHER.
HESTER.

HESTER.	**BUTCHER.**
Would you like to see my gold coin?	Ive brought you a present.

HESTER.
BUTCHER.

HESTER.	**BUTCHER.**
Before I give it to the Fund lemmie show you.	Its not much. Just meat. But its a good cut.

*(She holds up her coin. He shows a neatly tied
package.)*

HESTER.

Pretty aint it?

HESTER.
BUTCHER.

HESTER.	BUTCHER.
It was you who left the meat the other day.	Ive wanted you. For a long time.

(He gives her the package of meat.)

HESTER.

That was real nice. The meat. It cooked up good.

BUTCHER.

Yr lovely.

HESTER.

Oh, Im a regular princess, with my branded A—

BUTCHER.

I always figured you wanted to be alone—

HESTER.

—that weeps and stinks.

BUTCHER.

—but I figured I would try.

HESTER.

Dont make fun of me. "Yr lovely." Sure. Me and my bloody bloody apron.

BUTCHER.

(Rest.)

Theres no shame in a bloody apron.

HESTER.
BUTCHER.

(He takes her hand. She nervously takes it away.)

BUTCHER.

Whenever I see you yr always sitting or standing with yr left shoulder pulled back. Yr A is as plain as day but you dont want no one seeing it. You shouldnt be ashamed.

HESTER.

I dont like people staring.

BUTCHER.

Why do they brand you aborters? They dont brand us butchers.

HESTER.

The brand comes with the job is all I know. "And the brand must be visible at all times." Thats the law. Everyone knows what I do—but then, my A is also like a shingle and a license, so nobody in needll ever get suckered by a charlatan.

(Rest)

What we do is bad. And good. And bad and good and good and bad. Theres no easy way to look at it.

(Rest)

Go to prison or take this job. That was my choice. Choose A or choose B. I chose A.

BUTCHER.

You got a chance to get him out this way.

HESTER.

Thats the way I see it.

BUTCHER.

And you provide a service. You chose right.

HESTER.

Thank you.

BUTCHER.

You should put that coin in a safe place.

HESTER.

Good thinking.

> *(She looks around quickly and decides to put the coin in her shoe.)*

BUTCHER.

You must be excited about yr reunion picnic.

HESTER.

And a little nervous.

BUTCHER.

Its a wonder yll even recognize him, what with the time thats passed and the ways hes changed.

HESTER.

I'll know my Boy.

BUTCHER.

By his looks?

HESTER.

Better than that.

(Rest)

When they comed to take him away, just before they took him, I bit him. Hard. Right on the arm just here. I bit hard. Deep into his skin. His blood in my mouth. He screamed but then he was screaming anyway. After theyd tooked him away I went and bit myself. Just as hard and in the same place exactly. See the mark I got? My Boys got one too. Identical.

> *(She shows him her bite mark scar, on the inside of her left forearm, the remains of a horrid wound.)*

BUTCHER.

Hes a grown man now.

HESTER.

He'll always have my mark.

(Rest)

You think my A is ugly.

BUTCHER.

No.

HESTER.

But you could never love it.

BUTCHER.

Loving anything is hard.

HESTER.
BUTCHER.

> *(He takes her hand again. This time she doesnt pull away.)*

HESTER.

It would be nice. But you cant *spend the night.*

(Rest)

Too many people would see you leaving in the morning. You may not care but I care.

BUTCHER.

K.

> *(They sit there holding hands. The backdoor bell rings.)*

BUTCHER.

Yr bell.

HESTER.

(Rest)

Let it ring.

> *(The bell rings again, this time more insistently. HESTER makes no move to get up and answer it.)*

Scene Ten

(Hesters house. The next morning. Dawns early light. **MONSTER** *rummaging around Hesters front room looking for things to steal. He finds the meat, smells it and gobbles at it. Offstage* **HESTER** *begins singing. She sings a version of "Working Womans Song" to herself as she enters the room.* **MONSTER** *hears her and hides himself.)*

HESTER.

I LOVE WHAT WE DO WHEN WE DO IT WE DO IT
I FALL IN HIS ARMS AND HE PUTS ME THROUGH IT.
I TAKE HIS LOVE WITH NO COMPLAINING
HE TAKES MY LOVE, EVEN WHEN ITS RAINING...

*(***MONSTER*** grabs her.)*

MONSTER.

Gimmie all yr money and all yr food or I'll kill you.

HESTER.

I dont got much.

MONSTER.

Yve got hiding places. Ha! A gun!

(He spies a rusty shotgun above the mantel. Takes it down.)

MONSTER.

Its old. Does it work?

HESTER.

Sometimes. Its very rusty.

MONSTER.

Forget it.

(He tosses the gun down.)

MONSTER.

Wheres yr money at?

HESTER.
MONSTER.

MONSTER.
 Dont give it up and I'll kill you.

>   (**HESTER** *goes to a drawer, pulls it out, reaches
>   behind it, withdraws money, hands it to him.
>   As he takes the money from her he sees her
>   scar. He takes a good long look, then plays it
>   off.*)

HESTER.
MONSTER.

HESTER.
 Thats all.

MONSTER.
MONSTER.

HESTER.
 Thats all. On my life thats all.

MONSTER.
MONSTER.

HESTER.
 Yr staring at me.
MONSTER.
 No Im not.
HESTER.
 I gave you all my money.
MONSTER.
 Good.

(Rest)

I said I woulda killed you and I woulda. Just so you
know.

HESTER.
MONSTER.

> *(**MONSTER** hurries out the front door. **HESTER**
> stands as if rooted to the spot. Then, breathing
> a sigh of relief, she hurries to the window to
> make sure he is on his way. She then takes off
> her shoe and takes out the gold coin, holding
> it triumphantly up to the light.)*

Scene Eleven

(The HUNTERS *come in deep in conversation.)*

SECOND HUNTER.

I dont mind losing the bet. Not at all dont get me wrong.

THIRD HUNTER.

Thats why he bet you.

SECOND HUNTER.

Exactly. I knew I would lose.

FIRST HUNTER.

I dont get it.

THIRD HUNTER.

Reverse psychology.

SECOND HUNTER.

Exactly.

FIRST HUNTER.

Reverse psychology on who, on me?

SECOND HUNTER.

On the convict.

THIRD HUNTER.

Very smart.

FIRST HUNTER.

I dont get it.

THIRD HUNTER.

Hal was psyching out that convict.

FIRST HUNTER.

"Monster"!

THIRD HUNTER.

We shouldnt get on a first name basis with him.

FIRST HUNTER.

Why not? "Monster"! Im not scared to say his name. And we'll get real close to him soon enough—

SECOND HUNTER.

Cause I bet you. I bet you that he *wouldnt* come down. I place such a bet knowing Im an unlucky guy, and therefore knowing that I would more likely than not *lose* the bet and that me *losing* the bet would mean he was coming. Me betting you exerted a psychic pull on him.

THIRD HUNTER.

Hals bad luck works like a charm.

FIRST HUNTER.

Im giving you yr money back.

SECOND HUNTER.

Yr all right, Hank.

THIRD HUNTER.

Whens the last time we did a runthrough? You cant remember, right? Cause its been years.

FIRST HUNTER.

Its been years cause its lots of work.

THIRD HUNTER.

Its also a lot of fun.

SECOND HUNTER.

Whats a runthrough?

THIRD HUNTER.

The best thing to do to a convict when you catch him. It gets the loudest screams.

FIRST HUNTER.

You get a hot iron rod and run it up his bottom and out his throat.

THIRD HUNTER.

Then you stick the rod in the ground and let him wiggle on the stick.

SECOND HUNTER.

Shit.

FIRST HUNTER.

You wouldnt think they would wiggle for long but they do.

THIRD HUNTER.

And the screams—

SECOND HUNTER.

Im game to try if you all are.

THIRD HUNTER.

We're gonna find him, I can feel it. And besides getting rich off the money he'll make us, we'll have some fun.

FIRST HUNTER.

Say it come on say it.

SECOND HUNTER.

Monster!

THIRD HUNTER.

Monster!

SECOND & THIRD HUNTERS.

Monster! MONSTER!

FIRST HUNTER.

Come on lets get to work.

(They go on their way.)

Scene Twelve

> (**HESTER** *waiting. She wears a shawl that conceals her A. She looks at the sky and notes the time. She keeps waiting. She opens the picnic basket, examines the contents, closes the basket. She primps. She waits. She opens the basket, takes out a checked cloth and spreads it on the ground. She sits down on the cloth. Practices "meeting" her son.*)

HESTER.

He sees me on the ground like this he may think I shrunk. I'll stand.

(Rest)

"Son!" Too eager.

(Rest)

"Son." Not eager enough.

(Rest)

I look like Im waiting for a bus.

(Rest)

Kneeling. This is good. Kneeling in thanks. Put the past behind us and lets be thankful for this sunny picnic day—although he'll think Ive lost my legs. I'll stand.

> (*Far far away, a* **GUARD** *brings* **JAILBAIT** *out. They stand together. The* **GUARD** *wears a luncheon napkin at his chin and fills out paperwork on a clipboard.* **JAILBAIT** *wears shackles on his feet.*)

GUARD.

Just stand here. I'll take you to the picnic ground in a minute.

JAILBAIT.

Wheres she at?

GUARD.

Just behind that fence there.

(Rest)

You should be happy. Shes yr mother.

JAILBAIT.

What about my meal?

GUARD.

Shes bringing you a picnic. Real food. Yr lucky. I'll
come get you in an hour or so.

JAILBAIT.

Yr leaving me?

GUARD.

Its lunchtime for us too.

JAILBAIT.

You aint scared I'll make a run for it?

GUARD.

Youre wearing a chain. So if you run you wont run far.
Besides, yr moms visiting. And shes brought you a
picnic.

JAILBAIT.

I dont got no mom.

GUARD.

Sure you do. Everybodys got a mom. Even you.

*(The **GUARD** walks **JAILBAIT** toward **HESTER**.)*

Here he is, maam. Enjoy yrselves.

*(The **GUARD** goes back inside. She sees him
and they stand still, staring at each other.)*

HESTER.
JAILBAIT.
HESTER.
JAILBAIT.

HESTER.
(Son.)

JAILBAIT.
HESTER.

> *(He just looks at her, doesnt move. She walks to him. Hugs him gently then harder. He does not respond.)*

> *(She bursts into tears.)*

HESTER.
Waaaaahhhhhhhhhh!

JAILBAIT.
JAILBAIT.

> *(She cries for quite some time. He stands there, mildly interested, mostly bored.)*

HESTER.
Its you.

JAILBAIT.
I guess.

HESTER.
My child my love my son its you.

> *(She hugs him very hard. With some difficulty, he struggles free.)*

JAILBAIT.
They said you had food.

HESTER.
—Yes. I have food.

(Rest)

30 years. Well.

(Rest)

Lets see yr mark. The mark yr mother gave you all those years ago. People thought I was crazy. "I'll know my Boy anywhere," I said! Look at mine! See! My teeth marks! Yrs is identical! Lets see how it healed.

JAILBAIT.

Dont touch me.

HESTER.
JAILBAIT.

HESTER.

All these years locked up in this horrible place. "Don't touch me." Of course.

(Rest)

((Im going to get you out soon. Ive got friends with gold. But youve got to help. You keep befriending those bad people theyll keep blaming things on you. Make nice friends, son. Promise me.))

JAILBAIT.

Im hungry.

HESTER.

Of course yr hungry. See? A whole basket full of wonderful things. Lets see your arm. Just a peek.

JAILBAIT.

Hands off.

HESTER.

Oh.

JAILBAIT.

Can we eat, please?

(Rest)

Mother?

HESTER.

Waaaaaaah!

> *(She cries again. He grabs the basket and begins eating. She collects herself.)*

JAILBAIT.

I usually eat with my hands. Dya mind?

HESTER.

Not at all.

(He eats like an animal.)

Youve grown so much.

(Rest)

Yr such a man.

JAILBAIT.
HESTER.

JAILBAIT.

Thanks.

(He goes back to eating.)

HESTER.

Do I look old? Probably, right? But not too old I hope.

(Rest)

(Rest)

Lets see that mark I gave you. Just a quick look. I want to know what kind of scar its made. Take another look at mine. Kinda pretty, I think. I did them both in such a hurry but they turned out well. What do you think? Kind of looks like a heart. Like Im wearing my heart on my sleeve or something. Hahahahaha. Lemmie see yrs.

JAILBAIT.

Quit grabbing at me!

HESTER.

Sorry.

(Rest)

Could I pet you, son?

JAILBAIT.

Where?

HESTER.

On the head.

JAILBAIT.

Go ahead.

> *(She pets him very lightly on the head.)*

JAILBAIT.

Yr looking at me like you wanna eat me up.

HESTER.

Motherlove.

JAILBAIT.

Heavy.

(Rest)

What else you bring for me?

HESTER.

Cake.

JAILBAIT.

Show.

> *(He takes the entire cake and eats.)*

HESTER.

Look what living here has done to you. Eating yr food
with yr eyes scouring the countryside as if someones
gonna rush up and snatch yr goodies! Like this!

> *(She playfully snatches his food. He fiercely
> grabs it back.)*

HESTER.
JAILBAIT.

HESTER.

I brought wine.

JAILBAIT.

Break em open.

> *(She opens both bottles. He grabs them and gluts them down. Some of the wine makes it down his throat, some of it goes down his shirt.)*

JAILBAIT.

You know whatd be great? Lemmie put my head in yr lap and you tell me a story. Thatd be great.

HESTER.

Ok. Once upon a time you were little and I was young and everything was nice.

JAILBAIT.

And I wasnt bad?

HESTER.

You were never bad. They tell me yr bad but I dont believe them. You shouldnt believe them either.

(Rest)

Lets see yr mark.

> *(She gingerly searches his forearm. He lets her.)*

JAILBAIT.

You like looking at me dont you?

HESTER.

I thought I put it on the same arm I put mine on. Maybe I put it on the other. Its been a long time.

JAILBAIT.

You smell good. You wearing perfume?

> *(She goes to look at his other arm.)*

HESTER.

Im going to look at yr other arm, ok?

JAILBAIT.

I wanna look at your other arm.

(He rolls up her sleeve, bites her arm playfully. She laughs.)

HESTER.

Stop that! Now what are you doing?

(He is burying his face in her lap.)

HESTER.

Yr tickling me, son. Son, what are you doing?

JAILBAIT.

Im getting romantic. Yr picnic got me hot.

HESTER.

Stop that, son.

JAILBAIT.

That son crap may turn you on, lady, but it kinda breaks the mood for me, if you know what I mean.

HESTER.

Dont touch me like that.

JAILBAIT.

Yr not no virgin are you?

HESTER.

Stop it, baby.

JAILBAIT.

I aint no baby, Mama, Im a full grown man.

HESTER.

Theyd lock you up for good if they came out here and saw you getting fresh with your own mother.

JAILBAIT.

I love you.

HESTER.

Boy, stop that!

JAILBAIT.

Boy? I aint Boy. My names Joe.

HESTER.
JAILBAIT.

HESTER.

Yr not my son.

JAILBAIT.

Sorry. His names—

HESTER.

Boy. His name is Boy. Boy Smith.

JAILBAIT.

Funny name. I could say I never heard of him but I have.

(Rest)

(Rest)

Smashed his brains in myself. Hes dead.

(Rest)

I guess thats why they sent me to you in his place.

HESTER.

Dead.

JAILBAIT.

Bad things happen. All the time. But hey, no use crying.

HESTER.
HESTER.
HESTER.

JAILBAIT.

You gonna gimmie some or what?

HESTER.
HESTER.
HESTER.

JAILBAIT.

The way I see it we got ourselves some minutes left. And I always had a thing for older women.

(**JAILBAIT** *kisses her and feels her up.* **HESTER,** *struck dumb with grief and disbelief, lets* **JAILBAIT** *do what he wants. He touches and gropes her and she sits there, flicking at his hands from time to time as if she were flicking at flies. After a moment the action stops.* **HESTER** *sings "My Vengeance."*)

HESTER.
THE LOW ON THE LADDER,
THE BARRELS ROCK BOTTOM
WILL REACH UP AND STRANGLE
THE RICH, THEN GOD ROT THEM.
SHE'LL MOURN THE DAY
SHE CRUSHED US UNDERFOOT.
HER RICH GIRL WEALTH
WILL NOT STOP ME FROM PUTTING MY MARK ON HER,
AND IT WILL EQUAL WHAT WE'VE PAID.
MY VENGENCE WILL SHOW HER
HOW A TRUE MOTHER IS MADE.

(**JAILBAIT** *embraces her again and the rape continues.*)

PART TWO

Scene Thirteen

*(**MONSTER** and **FIRST LADY** sitting on that same park bench. Wanted posters of **MONSTER** hang all over the place. **MONSTER** smokes.)*

FIRST LADY.

I didnt know you smoked.

MONSTER.
FIRST LADY.

HESTER.

You got my note.

FIRST LADY.

Im here.

MONSTER.

I guess you got it.

(Rest)

You knocked up?

FIRST LADY.

No.

MONSTER.

You sure?

(Rest)

If yr knocked up its mine.

(Rest)

Keep it, okay? Something to remember me by.

FIRST LADY.

Im not—expecting.

MONSTER.

Too bad.

(Rest)

Whats yr husband do?

FIRST LADY.

Nothing.

MONSTER.

I seen yr house. Its a big house. Right in the middle of town. He must do something.

FIRST LADY.

Hes in business.

MONSTER.

I figured. A tycoon, right?

FIRST LADY.

Thats right. A tycoon.

MONSTER.

I want some money.

FIRST LADY.

How much.

MONSTER.

A lot. I wanna live in style. I dont see why I shouldnt, do you?

FIRST LADY.

How much.

MONSTER.

5 thousand coins.

FIRST LADY.

How about 3—

MONSTER.

How about 10. Thousand. 10 thousand.

(Rest)

Say its a deal. Come on. Agree. You cant con an ex-con.

FIRST LADY.

You were in prison.

MONSTER.

Yeah.

FIRST LADY.

Oh.

MONSTER.

Why you holding yr stomach. You knocked up?

FIRST LADY.

Im sick.

MONSTER.

Sure you arent knocked up?

FIRST LADY.

Yr the one theyre all looking for. Yr the man on the loose, arent you?

MONSTER.

You gonna snitch? You look like yr gonna snitch.

FIRST LADY.

Yr pictures all over town.

MONSTER.

You ever snitch?

FIRST LADY.

(Rest)

No.

MONSTER.

Good.

(Rest)

Hear the bells? Theyre ringing noon. The next time they ring 12 itll be midnight.

(Rest)

Bring me my money. 10 thousand coins. At midnight tonight.

FIRST LADY.

I'll turn you in.

MONSTER.

I'll kill you first. Believe it.

FIRST LADY.
MONSTER.

MONSTER.

12 midnight tonight. Go on. Get going. You got a lot of diamond rings to sell, Im sure. Thats it, hold yr stomach. I knocked you up, didnt I ? Didnt I?!

(She hurries away.)

Scene Fourteen

(Oustide Hesters back door. Two **WOMEN** *waiting.)*

WAITING WOMAN #1.

Weh noonka Flowmeh. Weh pak Nah rum—

WAITING WOMAN #2.

Weh nim ohnio Zamen die sah "noonka schwang," rum—

WAITING WOMAN #1.

Weh nam laisah sah Zamen. Woah-ya priceypricey eeh Beardkum der dak Zamensah like-a-rug woah.

WAITING WOMAN #2.

Tah humble.

WAITING WOMAN #1.

Tah humble si.

(Rest)

WAITING WOMAN #2.

Why dont she answer her bell?

WAITING WOMAN #1.

Sign says "Closed." Maybe she closed for good. Maybe she quit the business.

WAITING WOMAN #2.

I dont blame her. Mrs. Smith! Hey! Hey in there! Hey! Hey!

> **(FIRST LADY** *enters fresh from her encounter with* **MONSTER.** *She is heavily veiled and holds her stomach.)*

WAITING WOMAN #1.

Look.

WAITING WOMAN #2.

Well. A rich lady. Lah-dee-dah.

WAITING WOMAN #1.

Dont make fun.

(Rest)

Who is she you think?

WAITING WOMAN #2.

Who knows.

(Rest)

Ya come to Hester Smith cause she'll let you keep yr veil on and wont ask no questions, huh?

FIRST LADY.

Im here same as you.

WAITING WOMAN #1.

Loverboys seed growing inside you, huh?

WAITING WOMAN #2.

You got the guilties and needs to get rid of it before the husband finds out.

FIRST LADY.

Yes.

FIRST LADY.
FIRST LADY.
FIRST LADY.

(Rest)

FIRST LADY.

No. Not at all.

(Rest)

One seed is as good as another. And when the husband resembles the lover, he wont be none the wiser.

WAITING WOMAN #1.

Smart thinking.

WAITING WOMAN #2.

Real real smart thinking.

      (**FIRST LADY** *sings "My Little Enemy."*)

FIRST LADY.

>THEY SAY FIDELITY
>IS THE MOST IMPORTANT THING
>WHEN YR MARRIED.
>BUT ITS SUCH A PRICEY LUXURY.
>WHEN YR UP AGAINST THE WALL,
>YLL TAKE A POKE FROM SOME POOR SLOB.
>THE CHILD IM GROWING WILL BE MY SALVATION.
>WHO KNOWS, HE MAY GROW UP TO RULE THE NATION.
>AND MY HUSBAND, BLIND WITH HAPPINESS,
>WILL NEVER GUESS
>THE ENEMY IN HIS ARMY.

Thank you. Here. Spend this for me.

(She gives them money and goes.)

WAITING WOMAN #1.

Rich folk.

WAITING WOMAN #2.

Yeah.

Scene Fifteen

(Hesters home. She sits in a big tin tub.
CANARY *scrubs her back, giving her a bath.)*

CANARY.

Am I scrubbing you too hard?

HESTER.
HESTER.

CANARY.

Theyre reconciled again. Word is she went to her daddy
crying and he put out more money. And they spent last
night together. I lay in his bed waiting and he was with
her.

Oh, what money can do.

(Rest)

Warm water sweet soap and gentle scrubbing. Does it
feel good?

HESTER.

I could cut her head off.

CANARY.

Inhale. Soap smells good, dont it?

HESTER.

Youd put sleeping powder into her bedtime snack. I'd
sneak into her big house, find her room, and cut her
head off.

*(**HESTER***s backdoor bell rings.)*

CANARY.

Yr A is weeping. You got folks out there. 3 a minute ago
but now only 2. The "Closed" signs on the door. Hester
aint helping no one but herself today.

HESTER.

I could follow her on one of her afternoon constitutionals and jump out from behind a tree and strangle her with my bare hands.

CANARY.

Freedom Fund confirmed hes dead but I dont believe them and you shouldnt believe them neither. If hes dead whose been writing you all these years? Theyve just misplaced him. He'll turn up. Yll see.

HESTER.

Take my knife and stab her till theres nothing left of her but wounds. Then we'd be equal.

CANARY.

The Fund says yr due for a full refund.

(Rest)

I dont believe hes dead. But you could take the money anyway. You could retire.

HESTER.

I could slit her throat.

CANARY.

(Rest)

Do you know how many men and women they got locked up? More thans walking free in the streets thats how many. Its a wonder they aint lost them all. Prisoners get lost all the time, I'll bet. Sounds crazy but thats what kind of crazy world we live in. Something crazy happening every day. Like, just the other day, I seen yr mark. Not on you. On someone elses arm.

HESTER.

Whose?

(Rest)

Whose?!?!

HESTER.

CANARY.

CANARY.

—. Cant remember.

HESTER.

I'll get back at her. Im not a mother otherwise.

(Rest)

I'll get her. And yll help me.

CANARY.

Lemmie towel you off.

HESTER.

I'll get her and yll help me. We'll get her together.

CANARY.

We dont need to do nothing like that. We'll take our bad luck on the chin.

HESTER.

Take my bad luck on my chin. No. My chin aint big enough.

CANARY.

Lets get you dressed.

HESTER.

Yll help me.

CANARY.

No. If I help you I'd have to give up the Mayors bed. Theyd put all the blame on me. Anyway, what can we do? Just us 2?

HESTER.

I'll get Butcher to help. You and me and him makes 3. 3s the charm.

CANARY.

Idunno—

HESTER.

"Hes dead," they said. "According to our records, hes been dead for years," they said. "Sorry for the mix-up," they said. "Yll get a full refund," they said. A full refund aint enough.

(Rest)

Yll help me.

CANARY.

I'll help you. Whats the plan.

HESTER.

I dont got one yet.

CANARY.

Ah.

HESTER.

I'll think of something. And yll help.

CANARY.

(Rest)

Sure.

HESTER.

Good.

(The backdoor bell rings.)

HESTER.

(Rest)

Is tonight all right?

CANARY.

Tonight?!

HESTER.

Yes.

(The back bell rings again. And again.)

CANARY.
HESTER.
CANARY.
HESTER.

CANARY.

Tonights fine.

HESTER.

We'll kidnap her and toss her off a cliff! How does that
sound?

(Rest)

Wait here. Be ready. I'll talk to Butcher.

CANARY.

I remember whose arm it was. That Monster convict.
Remember I told you I saw him at the sea lookout?

HESTER.

Hes an evil person.

CANARY.

With a scar like yours.

HESTER.

Which goes to show that mothers all over the world bite
their sons. Boy tried to be good his whole life and now
his mother weeps. I wonder what that evil Monsters
mothers doing right now. Dancing, I bet.

(The bell rings again and again and again.)

I wont be gone for long. Be ready.

*(**HESTER** leaves. **CANARY** sits there.)*

Scene Sixteen

(The HUNTERS *walk across the stage.)*

FIRST HUNTER.

Peoplev seen em.

THIRD HUNTER.

That streetwalker gave us a piece of his shirt.

SECOND HUNTER.

Plus that anonymous tip: "ocean overlook at midnight."

FIRST HUNTER.

We'll catch him before morning. The dogs have the scent.

THIRD HUNTER.

Cept theyre going around in circles.

SECOND HUNTER.

We'll catch him tonight. We'll show him what it means to be a Hunter.

(They continue on their way.)

Scene Seventeen

(Butchers place. Meat hanging around on meat hooks. **BUTCHER** *at his butchers block hacking away at a piece of meat.* **HESTER** *sitting there watching.)*

BUTCHER.

This is violent. I know. It must be upsetting to you after everything thats happened. Its an order for Hizzoner.

HESTER.

You delivering it?

BUTCHER.

Hes picking it up himself. Its his day to rub shoulders with the people.

HESTER.

I dont want him to rub my shoulder.

BUTCHER.

Stand over there when he comes. He wont notice you.

(Rest)

I was on my way over. I got some flowers for you back in the meat cooler. You should be in bed—

HESTER.

I need yr help.

BUTCHER.

Ask away. Wait: here he comes.

(As **HESTER** *steps into the shadows, the* **MAYOR** *enters with his basket.)*

BUTCHER.

Good to see you, sir.

MAYOR.

The local butcher at his chopping block. Hard honest worker. Thats what I like to see.

BUTCHER.

Ive got yr order right here.

MAYOR.

Im passing out cigars. Have one.

BUTCHER.

Thank you.

MAYOR.

My First Lady and I are expecting. A child.

HESTER.

(A child.)

MAYOR.

You heard right.

HESTER.

(A child!)

MAYOR.

Thats right. She begged me to keep it hush-hush but I cant help myself. I feel that its my duty to share the news.

BUTCHER.

Congratulations.

HESTER.

(A child!)

MAYOR.

My wife with child. That makes me a father.

BUTCHER.

Congratulations.

HESTER.

(A child.)

MAYOR.

I want to weep.

HESTER.

((You will.))

MAYOR.

Whadyasay?

BUTCHER.

Nothing.

(*Rest*)

Yr meat.

MAYOR.

Thank you. Until next week.

BUTCHER.

Until next week.

(**MAYOR** *leaves.* **HESTER** *comes out of hiding.*)

BUTCHER.

They finally got lucky.

HESTER.
HESTER.

BUTCHER.

Hester?

HESTER.

Sweetheart.

BUTCHER.

I wish them luck.

HESTER.

So do I.

BUTCHER.

After everything thats happened?

HESTER.

I wish them luck.

BUTCHER.

Yr an angel.

HESTER.

I need yr help.

BUTCHER.

Anything my angel wants. But first:

(*Rest*)

I earn a good living. And I still have my looks. There are a lot of women who wink at the Meat Man and I know what theyre thinking. Word is Im a catch.

(He stands at his butcher block and sings "A Meat Man is a Good Man to Marry.")

A MEAT MAN IS A GOOD MAN TO MARRY.
THE WIFE OF A MEAT MAN DONT WORRY
THE CHILDREN WILL NEVER GO HUNGRY,
ALWAYS PLENTY OF MEAT IN THE TUMMY.

A MEAT MAN, HIS LIVESTOCK ARE FRIENDLY.
THEY GO TO THE SLAUGHTER FULL KNOWING
HE WILL KILL THEM AND CARVE THEM MOST KINDLY,
IN OUR STOMACHS THEYLL HELP US KEEP GROWING.

WITH ME YR MATE, EVERYDAY WE'LL HAVE STEAK,
GIZZARDS, CHITTLINS AND CHOPS.

COME ON, LETS TIE THE KNOT.
PORK, BEEF, MUTTON, YLL BE MY ONLY ONE,
PIG TAILS AND FEET AND SNOUTS,
WE'LL KISS DAY IN AND OUT.
MAKE ME YR BALL AND CHAIN,
WE'LL DINE ON FRIED BRAIN.

AND WHAT COULD EVER BEAT A HONEY-DEAR
WHO CAN MAKE A SILK PURSE FROM A SOW'S EAR?

THE WIFE OF A MEAT MAN IS HAPPY.
ALL HER DAYS ARE SO SUNNY AND EASY.
ALL HER NIGHTS FULL OF HOT HEAVY BREATHING
AND LOVE,
CAUSE A MEAT MANS THE BEST MAN TO MARRY.

BUTCHER.
HESTER.

(He leaves his butcher block and comes over to her.)

BUTCHER.

Marry me.

HESTER.

I need yr help. With the First Lady.

(Rest)

I wanna talk to her is all.

BUTCHER.

And you want me to help you think of what to say.

HESTER.

Shes shy about being seen with me. Her position, you know and everything thats happened. She wants to come to my house but dont want no one to know.

(Rest)

I need you to drive your truck. Tonight. Say some of the order was forgotten and yr delivering it. Canary will be waiting there with her. The First Lady aint been feeling well as of late so she may be—foggy, but dont let that stop you. Dont let nothing stop you. She wants to talk tonight. Shes real insistent. And she dont want no one knowing. Bring her to me, let us talk then take her home again thats all.

BUTCHER.

Whatll you talk about?

HESTER.

Just chitchat. Woman to woman stuff. I have a feeling she wants to apologize. Maybe even give me some sort of—payment for my hardships. Go get her around 11. Itll be dark. No onell see. Then take her home around midnight.

(Rest)

We need to have a talk, her and me, thats all, just a talk, woman to woman, her and me. Yll help?

BUTCHER.

Sure.

(Rest)

Then we'll get married.

HESTER.

Then we'll get married.

> *(He tries to hug her. She gently pulls away.)*

HESTER.

Mmnot ready for touching yet. I need to go home.

BUTCHER.

I'll walk you.

HESTER.

No thanks.

(Rest)

After me and her talk. We can be together then.

> *(He tries to kiss her cheek. She goes. He goes back to his chopping block but just stands there.)*

Scene Eighteen

(**3 FRESHLY FREED PRISONERS** *singing "Hard Times."*)

FRESHLY FREED PRISONERS.
I DONE HARD TIME ON THIS EARTH.
HARD TIME ON THE ROCK PILE.
HARD TIME BEHIND THE BARS,
AND NOW AT LAST IM HOME.

IS THERE A FACE THAT KNOWS MY FACE?
A VOICE THAT KNOWS MY NAME?
HARD TIMES IN THESE FREE STREETS
IF NO ONE WELCOMES ME.

HARD TIMES, HARD TIMES,
HARD TIMES, HARD TIMES,
HARD TIMES, IF YA FOLLOWED ME THIS FAR,
I'LL JUST LAY DOWN AND DIE.

Scene Nineteen

(Hesters place. Its dark. The room is dimly lit. She readies her tools.)

HESTER.

Ready yr tools, Hester. Prepare yr instruments. Sharpen yr knives, clean yr hoses, boil yr water, check the strength of yr straps. Itll be easy. She wont feel nothing. Not right away. And she'll wake up tomorrow bloody and wondering whered the baby go? But no. She wont know.

(Rest)

Rip her child from her like she ripped mine from me.

(Rest)

Shes expecting. But shes not expecting this.

(Someone stands in her back doorway.)

HESTER.

Im closed tonight. Yll have to come back tomorrow.

*(**MONSTER** comes in.)*

HESTER.

Tell yr wife Im closed.

MONSTER.

Im lost.

HESTER.

I cant help you tonight.

MONSTER.

I got out of prison just now. You heard us singing.

HESTER.

I heard. Huh. You look familiar. A little. Im real busy just now—

MONSTER.

I got out of jail alive. Ive got the personal effects of a friend of mine who died in there. I promised him I'd bring them to his mother. They gave me directions but I lost my way.

HESTER.

Where ya headed?

MONSTER.

"The Rich Girls House." She must be a rich woman now but "The Rich Girls House" was all he said.

HESTER.

Go back to the square. Someonell point the way.

MONSTER.

My friends mother. She works for them. Scrubbing floors.

HESTER.

Scrubbing floors.

MONSTER.

Yeah.

(Rest)

He was Smith. Her too.

(Rest)

Why are you staring?

HESTER.

No reason.

MONSTER.

Yr circling me.

HESTER.

You look familiar.

MONSTER.

Yr busy. I'll leave you—

HESTER.

Wait! His effects. Lemmie see. Just a peek. Im curious.

MONSTER.

Theres not much. Just a tin cup. And a spoon. See?

(He shows her the cup and spoon.)

HESTER.

(Rest)

Tin cup and spoon, you dont look like Boy Smith at all but yll have to be enough to remember him by.

(Rest)

Dear son. This is all thats left.

(Rest)

Im his mother. Im his dead mother because hes dead.

MONSTER.

He told me you worked at the Rich—

HESTER.

The dead Boys dead mother works for herself now. Shes an aborter. Dont hang yr head shes not yr mom. My fucking A. He woulda hated what his mother has become.

MONSTER.

No.

(Rest)

I'll tell you stories about him.

HESTER.

Not now. Its a busy night for me.

(Rest)

My A. My tin cup. My spoon. And you. I know you.

MONSTER.

Yr sons alive.

HESTER.

I heard you described.

MONSTER.

He needs yr help.

HESTER.

Posters hung all over town.

MONSTER.

Hes as alive as I am.

HESTER.

Yr Monster! Help! Help!

MONSTER.

Quiet!

HESTER.

Let go of me! Help!

MONSTER.

Shut up! Shut up!

>   *(He subdues her.)*

Look. My mark.

(Rest)

You marked me years ago. Its just like yours. Look.

HESTER.

I marked my *son*. He was good and then he died. Youve got an ugly scar and yr looking for a hiding place.

MONSTER.

The letters you wrote him—me. Ive got them all.

HESTER.

Because he gave them to you.

MONSTER.

Because you wrote them to me. I know them all by heart. I'll recite, you read along.

HESTER.

Cant. Dont need to. Monster. *Evil!* Thats what you are. Ive heard the news. Go on, kill me! Do whatever it is you do! Get it over with!

>   *(He releases her.)*

MONSTER.

(Rest)

Mother.

>   *(She hurriedly takes up her old shotgun and points it at him.)*

HESTER.

My son was good. This is a gun. Run.

> *(She backs him toward the back door and he runs off. She puts the gun down and goes over to the table to examine the tin cup, the spoon and those letters. Butchers truck is heard pulling up.)*

Trinkets. Maybe from my Boy, maybe not.

(Rest)

My mark looks like a heart. His looked horrid. Like a gash.

> *(**CANARY** and **BUTCHER** at the front door. They hold **FIRST LADY** between them.)*

Come in before yr seen.

> *(**BUTCHER** and **CANARY** come in escorting a groggy **FIRST LADY**.)*

BUTCHER.

Shes ill.

HESTER.

Its probably just a dizzy spell.

CANARY.

Lets sit her in the chair.

> *(They sit her down.)*

BUTCHER.

Looks worse than a dizzy spell.

HESTER.

The rich get dizzy all the time. And the richer they are the dizzier they get.

FIRST LADY.

He wanted money but I snitched. Ha.

BUTCHER.

Shes been saying that the whole ride.

FIRST LADY.

I snitched I snitched I snitched.

HESTER.

Come with me, madam. Right this way. Come in here and we'll have our talk.

BUTCHER.

I'll help you—

HESTER.

Ive got her. Canary, keep Butcher company.

CANARY.

Whats this stuff here?

HESTER.

Just some garbage.

CANARY.

Theyre letters you wrote to Boy. Says so right here.

HESTER.
CANARY.

FIRST LADY.

I snitched. I snitched.

CANARY.

Jamah, Hester, jamah?

HESTER.

Doht.

CANARY.

Jamah?

BUTCHER.

No fair you two Talking in front of me. Uh, *noonka Talking-mehnavee.* No fair.

HESTER.

A friend of his brought them by. *Le traja Scrapeahdepth woah-ya, C-Mary.*

CANARY.

Scrapeahdepth?

HESTER.

Di.

FIRST LADY.

I snitched. I snitched.

BUTCHER.

Dont mind me, I'll just sit here. Wheres yr radio?

HESTER.

Stolen.

CANARY.

*Cha Eyeyaya s eh cha Muka vee chet-la Scrapeahdepth
ey cocodi Scrapeahdepth. Hester—*

HESTER.

Chet-la eye brack zeemeh. Zeemeh.

CANARY.

HESTER.

CANARY.

HESTER.

> *(The churchbells announce the hour. 12
> midnight.)*

HESTER.

Ha! You see what motherlove can do? Get in yr head
and make you see all sorts of things.

(Rest)

Come on, maam. Entertain yrselves, we'll be quick.

> *(**HESTER** and **FIRST LADY** go into the back
> room, leaving **BUTCHER** and **CANARY**.)*

CANARY.

She'll open the back door. The fresh airll perk her right
up.

BUTCHER.

What were you two talking about?

CANARY.

This and that.

BUTCHER.

She looked troubled.

CANARY.

Shes just tired.

BUTCHER.

Whatdoyathink theyre talking about?

CANARY.

Womens things. Private womens things. Motherhood things. Things like that. Not for the likes of me to hear. Or you.

(Rest)

Have a drink. I'll rub yr feet.

> *(He drinks. After removing his socks and shoes she rubs his feet.)*

BUTCHER.

You never had a child?

CANARY.

Not yet.

BUTCHER.

You oughta get married.

CANARY.

Naw. Not me.

BUTCHER.

Letters she wrote her son. Poor thing.

CANARY.

Love her a lot. Love her so much that yr lovell fill up the wound shes got. Give it a try, K?

BUTCHER.

I plan to.

> *(**FIRST LADY** from offstage:)*

FIRST LADY.

Oh!

> (**BUTCHER** *begins to move toward the back room.* **CANARY** *stops him.*)

CANARY.

Dont go in there. Sit here with me. Keep me company. You ever had yr soles read? Lets see: yll live a long life.

BUTCHER.

Will I get married?

CANARY.

And live happily forever.

BUTCHER.

Whats she doing in there?

CANARY.

Talking. Let them Talk.

(Rest)

Stay here with me. Please.

BUTCHER.
CANARY.

> (**FIRST LADY** *from offstage:*)

FIRST LADY.

Oh!

CANARY.

Read the letters to me. Go on. We're her friends. Lets pass the time.

BUTCHER.

"Dear Son, yr 12 today. Thats a lot of years. I thought you would be out long before now. Every time I go to the Fund theres another excuse. What can you do? I take it on the chin and you should too because I know that you get points for good behavior. Next year yll be

13 and back at home and we will spend the next 13 years having one big long birthday party! Wont that—"

(**HESTER** *comes out. In her haste she forgot to put on her apron and so her dress and hands are stained with blood. She stands there. Horrific.*)

(*And trumphant. She tosses her bloody tools in her wash bucket, lights a candle.*)

CANARY.

Taht?

HESTER.

Taht.

(**CANARY** *gives* **HESTER** *a kiss on the cheek. Its goodbye.*)

CANARY.

Hester, weh Seven-leagues swich tue ee meh. Ya weh tahrum sah Dinkydow, eh?

HESTER.

I understand.

CANARY.

Eee sah Le traja scrapeahdepth. Ki bunda-ley?

HESTER.

Weh race. Pabala weh fihnder. Pabala.

CANARY.

(*Rest*)

I guess we can take her home now?

HESTER.

Please.

(**CANARY** *goes to load* **FIRST LADY** *into the truck.* **BUTCHER** *puts on his shoes and stands there ready to go.* **HESTER** *gets her basket.*)

HESTER.
BUTCHER.
HESTER.
BUTCHER.

> (As **BUTCHER** *turns to follow* **CANARY** *he passes* **HESTER**, *and she takes his hand. Her blood-smeared hand bloodies his hand. They hold hands for a moment and then he lets her hand go and, walking out through the back room, very thoroughly wipes the blood off onto his pants.* **HESTER** *stands there with her basket.*)

HESTER.
HESTER.
HESTER.

> (*After a moment his truck is heard pulling off.* **HESTER** *hurries around the room stuffing things into her basket.*)

HESTER.
Hes not. He couldnt be. But what if he is. Monster. He isnt. But he could be. Although hes not. You know hes not. Just wanna make sure. See that mark again. Yr motherlove is playing with yr mind, thats all. Or it is him. Maybe. What does a monster need. Food. Money. Clothes. More money. I'll get Butcher to hide him. He wont like the idea at first cause hes law abiding but lovell take care of that. Maybe. Butcherll hide him good. Somehow.

> (*We can hear dogs barking in the distance.* **MONSTER** *is standing in her front doorway.*)

MONSTER.
Mother.

HESTER.
MONSTER.

MONSTER.
Mother.

HESTER.
MONSTER.

MONSTER.
Mother.
HESTER.
Son.
MONSTER.
Theyre on my trail.
HESTER.
Why would anyone want to catch you?
MONSTER.
Theyve got my scent. She snitched. One of the dogs bit me. But I had my knife and got him good. They bit me but I cut them. I ran but their blood and my blood—. Mother?
Mother?
HESTER.
Yr all grown up. Yr bleeding.
MONSTER.
Theyre bleeding too.
HESTER.
We'll turn out the lights and theyll think nobodys home and theyll go away. Theyll go look somewheres else. Theyll go away. Theyll go away wont they?
MONSTER.
I dont think so.
HESTER.
Theyll come to the door and I'll tell them I aint seen you. "What the hell would I be doing seeing a villian

like that," I'll say. Then theyll go away. Then yll run out the back.

MONSTER.

They wont go away. Theyre hunters. They hunt. They can smell me. Theyre hunters and they can smell me. They wont go away. Theyll do what they got to do to catch the Monster.

HESTER.
MONSTER.

HESTER.

You used to be so good. What happened?

MONSTER.

Oh—this and that.

(Rest)

Better a monster than a boy. I made something of myself. It wasnt hard.

(He sings "The Making of a Monster.")

YOUD THINK ITD BE HARD
TO MAKE SOMETHING HORRID.
ITS EASY.
YOUD THINK IT WOULD TAKE
SO MUCH WORK TO CREATE
THE DEVIL INCARNATE.
ITS EASY.
THE SMALLEST SEED GROWS TO A TREE,
A GRAIN OF SAND PEARLS IN AN OYSTER.
A SMALL BIT OF HATE IN A HEART WILL INFLATE,
AND THATS MORE SO MUCH MORE THAN ENOUGH
TO MAKE YOU A MONSTER.
YOUD THINK ITD BE HARD
TO MAKE SOMETHING HORRID.
ITS EASY.

(The sound of dogs barking gets louder.)

When they catch me theyll hurt me. Run me through and plant me in yr front yard so you can hear me scream. They catch me and theyll run me through. You hide me theyll run you through too. I wonder how much itll hurt? Theyll keep me alive and cut me up and I wonder how much itll hurt?

(Rest)

Hear the dogs? Take the gun. Shoot me with it.

HESTER.

Dont be silly.

MONSTER.

Us killing me is better than them killing me.

HESTER.

You were always so silly.

(The sound of dogs barking gets louder.)

MONSTER.

I heard once how they cut one guys balls off and let him watch the dogs eat them and then they cut his fingers off and the dogs ate those and he had to watch. His fingers and then his toes then his feet then his hands.

(Rest)

Please.

HESTER.
HESTER.

MONSTER.

Please.

> *(The sound of the dogs barking is very loud. The **HUNTERS** voices are heard. **HESTER** and **MONSTER** sit close together. They hold their arms side by side comparing their bite marks.)*

HESTER.
MONSTER.
HESTER.
MONSTER.
HESTER.
MONSTER.

HESTER.

I have a way to do it that wont hurt.

(Rest)

Give me yr knife. Sit in my lap.

> *(She sits in a chair. He hands her his knife
> and sits on the floor in front of her with his
> back toward her stomach. She gently pets his
> head. Then, with a quick firm motion, she
> slits his throat like* **BUTCHER** *taught her. He
> dies. She holds him in her lap. The sound of
> dogs barking and* **HUNTERS** *voices are now
> deafening. Theyre right outside her door.
> They force their way in. They stand around
> looking at* **HESTER** *and* **MONSTER.** *The dogs
> bay outside.)*

FIRST HUNTER.

Its him!

SECOND HUNTER.

But hes dead!

THIRD HUNTER.

Too bad!

FIRST HUNTER.

Plenty of fun still to be had, though!

THIRD HUNTER.

Hes still warm.

(Rest)

Hes ours by rights, gal. Give him up.

FIRST HUNTER.

   If you think yll get any of the reward money, you got
   another thing coming.

> (*The* **HUNTERS** *leave dragging* **MONSTERS**
> *body.* **HESTER** *sits there alone. She gets up,*
> *drops the knife in the wash bucket. She lights*
> *another candle. She sits down.*)

HESTER.
HESTER.
HESTER.

> (**HESTER** *sings* "*Working Womans Song –*
> *Reprise.*")

HESTER.

   I DIG MY DITCH WITH NO COMPLAINING,
   WORK IN THE HOT SUN, OR EVEN WHEN ITS RAINING.
   AND WHEN THE BITTER DAY FINALLY COMES TO AN END,
   THEYLL SAY—

> (*She sits there unable to continue.*)

HESTER.
HESTER.
HESTER.

> (*After a moment, the backdoor bell rings*
> *insistently. She ignores it. It rings again,*
> *more insistently. She gets up and puts on her*
> *apron, then wearily sits back down. After a*
> *moment the bell rings again.*)

HESTER.
HESTER.
HESTER.

(She gets up, picks up her tools and goes back to work.)

End of Play

TALK TRANSLATION

Part One,
Scene One
Page 1

die Abah-nazip.	The abortion.

Page 3

Die la-sah Chung-chung? woah-ya.	...And her pussy? Her pussy is so disgusting, so slack, so very very completely dried out.
seh turn... woah-ya	Yr pussy is all dried out
teeh tum-a... oromakeum!	You got a respectable good-for-nothing vagina!

Page 7

falltima... woah-ya.	When her period comes she is in hysterics.

Page 9

die Abah-nazip.	The abortion.

Scene Two,
Pages 11-12

Papameh! ... ma-Ovo!	Pity me! I got my period again!
Meh Kazo-say... ee—	My vagina is nice and pleasant and—

Scene Three,
Page 16

die Abah-nazip.	The abortion.
tee-tee... Zoo.	They open their legs for anybody and everybody.
Hee la... nice-like.	As if their vaginas were their mouths.

Hi-Chungwoah! ... Baza	Their vaginas are like common sewers.
Woah-ya dateh.	I totally agree with you.

Scene Five,
Page 28

Le doe-dunk... hunter.	You force yrself on yr wife and then you send her to me, Mister Hunter.

Scene Six,
Page 32

Suptah nekkie... Noonke!	You and yr slack dried-up prissy pussy! No one would be caught dead inside such a stupid twat! May you never conceive! May yr womb dry up and shrivel! May yr tubes tie themselves in knots! May yr egg sacks be forever empty! May yr breasts shrivel and never ever give milk!

Scene Seven,
Page 34

kaltie Bleehc	Chilly twat

Weh noonka... rum—	I missed my period. I stuck something up there, but—
Weh nim... rum— Weh nam... woah.	I took one of them tests. It said "not pregnant," but—
	I dont bother with the tests. Theyre so expensive and my man says, they lie anyway.
Tah humble.	Yr showing.
Tah humble si.	Yr showing too.

Scene Nineteen,
Pages 92-3

Jamah, Hester, jamah?	Hester, whats the matter?
Doht.	Nothing.
Jamah?	What is it?
noonka... mehnavee.	I couldnt speak TALK to save my life.
Le traja... C-Mary	He had a very odd-looking scar.
Scrapeahdepth?	An odd-looking scar?
Di.	Yeah.
Cha Eyeyaya... Hester.	The look on yr face says the scar wasnt just any scar, Hester—
Chet-la... Zeemeh.	It looked like mine, it did. It did.

Taht?	Is it done?
Taht.	Its done.
Hester, weh... Dinkydow, eh?	Im going to have to keep my distance from you for a while. To avoid suspicion, you understand?
Eee sah... bunda-ley?	What will you do about the man with the odd looking scar?
Weh race... Pabala.	I'll dash out of here. Maybe I'll find him. Maybe.

www.ingramcontent.com/pod-product-compliance
Lightning Source LLC
Chambersburg PA
CBHW070627120726
47909CB00004B/1350